Oak Brook Public Library
1112 Oak Brook Road
Oak Brook, Illinois 60521
990-2222

haiku by J. Patrick Lewis

Black Swan White Crow

woodcuts by Chris Manson

ATHENEUM BOOKS FOR YOUNG READERS

To Jon Lanman
—J. P. L.

For Patricia
—C. M.

Atheneum Books for Young Readers
An imprint of Simon & Schuster Children's Publishing Division
1230 Avenue of the Americas
New York, New York 10020

Book design by Chris Manson
The illustrations and poems were cut in wood and printed by Chris Manson.
Manufactured in the United States of America

10 9 8 7 6 5 4 3 2 1

Library of Congress Cataloging-in-Publication Data
Lewis, J. Patrick.
Black swan/white crow / by J. Patrick Lewis : illustrated by Chris Manson.
p. cm.
Summary: A collection of thirteen haiku with themes from nature and the outdoors.
ISBN 0-689-31899-5
1. Nature—Juvenile poetry. 2. Children's poetry, American. 3. Haiku, American.
[1. Nature—Poetry. 2. American poetry. 3. Haiku.] I. Manson, Christopher, ill. II. Title.
PS3562.E9465B53 1995
811´.54—dc20 94-34984 CIP AC

Haiku seems as Japanese as cherry blossoms in spring. And why not? Centuries ago, Japan gave birth to haiku (meaning "beginning phrase"), and there it was nurtured by its most renowned masters—Basho, Buson, Issa, and Shiki. Like other forms of poetry, haiku has traveled well and widely, welcomed the world over by poets who have adapted it to their own languages.

Originally, this short poem lived by strict rules. For example, haiku should be seventeen syllables long, in three lines (5-7-5), and should always contain a "season word," like summer or autumn, or a symbol of the season—say, March crocuses or a sudden snowstorm. But seventeen syllables in Japanese is roughly equal to twelve—some say nine—syllables in English. And many haiku writers today go beyond the strict use of a season word to include almost anything in the natural world as fair game for their poetry.

You can too. To write a haiku, you might go for a walk in a city park, a meadow, the zoo. Put all of your senses on full alert. Watch. Listen. Imagine that what you are seeing or smelling or hearing has never been seen, smelled, or heard before—and may never be again. Now take a picture of it—but only with your words.

The best haiku make you think and wonder for a lot longer than it takes to say them.

J. P. L.

The meadow reddens—
my old black lab fills
the sky with quail

Knee-deep in salmon,
buckleaping upstream—
grizzly bear in paradise

Spring hurries by—
the small brown house
raises the roof

Plains blizzard!
Bison, shoulder to shoulder—
music of sleet and slow tongues

Blue patches of noon—
the crows *caw-caw*ling
on the telephone wire

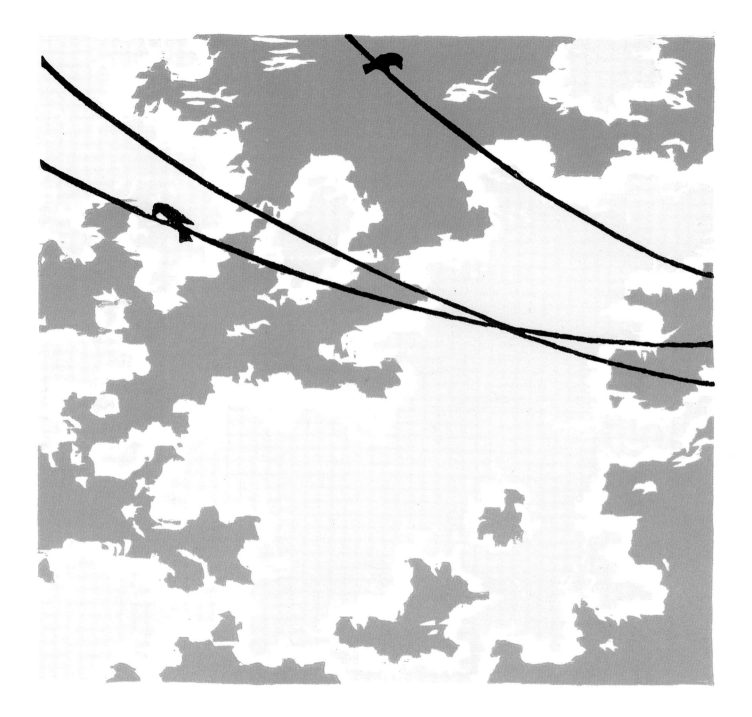

Frantic sandpiper—
high tides erasing
her footnotes

Skeleton elms
clicking above two deer
at the saltlick...a crowd

The spider yo-yos
down August to a hemlock
petalworth of shade

Snowdrifts to his knees,
a scarecrow left with nothing
up his sleeve

O little white crow,
have you seen my brother,
the black sheep?

After the storm, wild horses
thunder through tide pools—
their own rain

Thanksgiving Day...
Indian corn whispering
in the pilgrim cold

Out of the morning mist
a black swan sailing—
no longer alone.

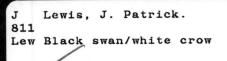